Jump Frog Jump

When Olga found Wilbur, a fine big frog, in the lot next door, it was her brother Henry who announced that he would take Wilbur to the annual Jump Frog celebration.

Papa considered the matter and decided that Henry could enter Wilbur in the contest, but the winnings should be divided equally between Henry and Olga.

Wilbur was trained for distance jumping, and at last the day of the event arrived.

Patricia Miles Martin has invented some wonderful adventures for Olga, Henry and Wilbur, concerned with the annual Frog Jump Contest in Calaveras County, in California.

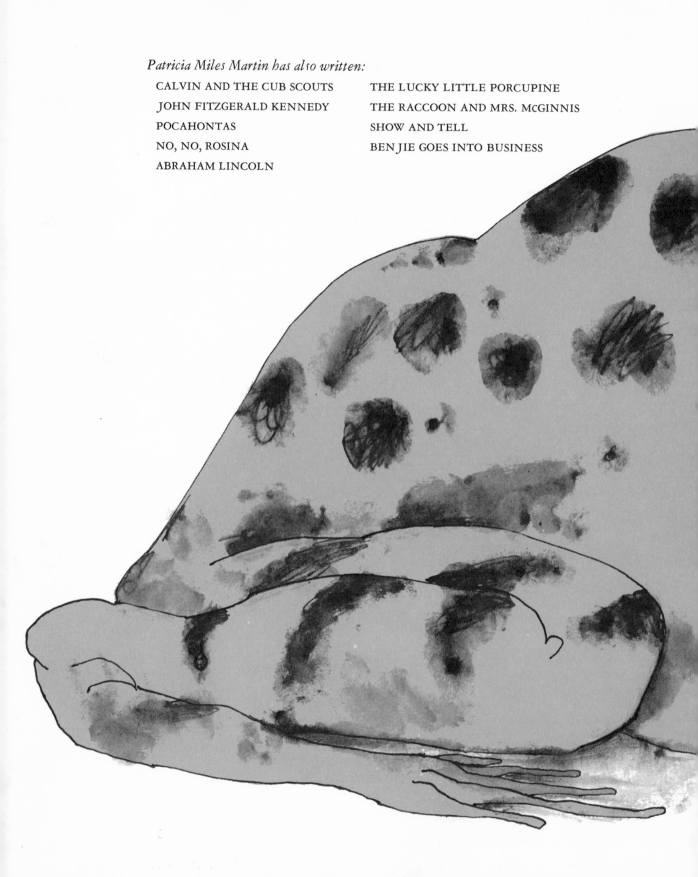

Patricia Miles Martin has also written:

CALVIN AND THE CUB SCOUTS

JOHN FITZGERALD KENNEDY

POCAHONTAS

NO, NO, ROSINA

ABRAHAM LINCOLN

THE LUCKY LITTLE PORCUPINE

THE RACCOON AND MRS. McGINNIS

SHOW AND TELL

BEN JIE GOES INTO BUSINESS

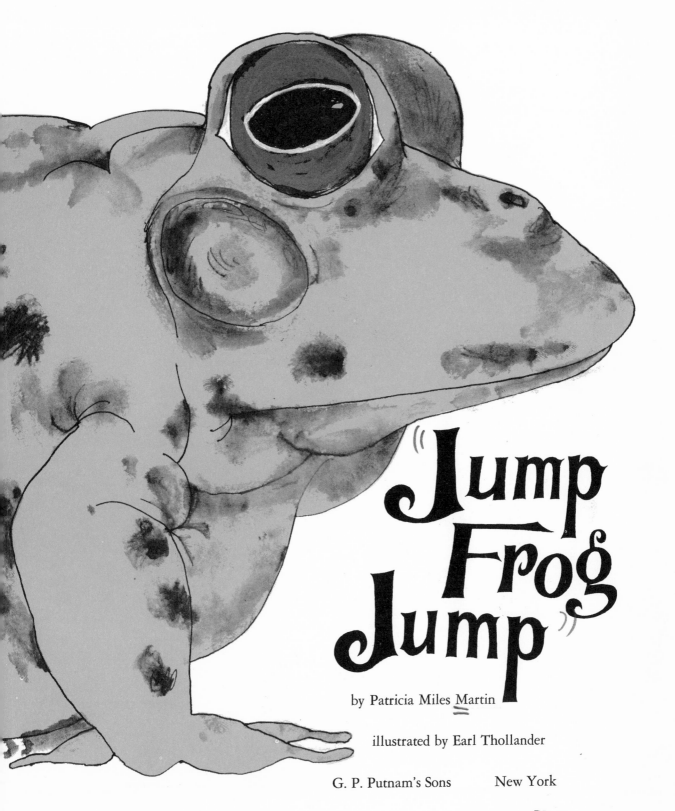

Jump Frog Jump

by Patricia Miles Martin

illustrated by Earl Thollander

G. P. Putnam's Sons   New York

To Patricia Gallagher

ver since Olga and Henry heard Papa read Mark Twain's famous story about the jumping frog of Calaveras County, they each wanted a frog.

"I'm not exactly comfortable about having a frog around the house," said Mama. "How about having a pair of canaries? Or a goldfish?"

"I'd rather have a frog," Olga said.

"Same here," said Henry.

Papa had told them about the Jumping Frog contest that was part of the yearly fair at Angel's Camp in Calaveras County. That was one of the exciting things about living in California. It wasn't far to go to the fair.

"They hold that Jump Frog Jubilee each year and it's just like the jump that Mark Twain wrote about, a hundred years ago," said Papa. "And the whole fair is fun. People come from all over the United States to see it."

"I'd like to go," Henry said. "I'd take my own frog."

Once, Henry and Olga went hunting down by the
creek just outside of town, and they hunted all after-
noon.

They came home with five pollywogs and one
garter snake.

"Wrong time of year, maybe," said Papa.

"Or perhaps the wrong creek," said Mama.

Olga kept looking.

And one morning, she heard something and could hardly believe her ears. It sounded like a frog croaking. She was almost sure it was a frog. It was a deep, rumbling croak, and it came from the back of the vacant lot next door where the blackberries grew.

She worked her way through the jungle of thorns and there he was, swimming in an old discarded tub that was half full of rain water.

She carried him to the kitchen door. "Look what I found," she said.

"Where'd you find him?" Henry asked.

"I found him in the blackberry bushes. He lives in an old tub. And he can jump higher than this—" Olga measured with her hand.

Henry galloped off, but he came back empty-handed. "I thought there might be another one there," he said. "But there wasn't. I'll train this one and take him to the fair."

"No you won't," Olga said. "I found him. Wilbur's mine."

Henry roughed her hair and shoved his face close to hers. "No little old girl is going to take Wilbur to the Frog Jump," he said.

At this point, Olga hit Henry.

Now, she sat in the kitchen on a high stool and faced the corner of the room. She was being punished. Since there was nothing else to do, she counted the ivy leaves on the wallpaper vine, and thought about Wilbur. She felt a tear wobbling down the side of her nose and she hooked her toes around the rungs of the stool. She wished that she had hit Henry harder.

A car door slammed outside, and she knew this was Papa coming home from the office and he would ask why she was being punished. She would tell him, and he would probably say that neither she nor Henry could take Wilbur to the fair.

I wish I hadn't hit Henry, she thought.

The door opened, and Papa's voice boomed out.

"Well, well, well. I see that Olga is in the corner again. And what happened this time?"

Olga turned around to explain. "Henry said that *he* is going to take Wilbur to the Frog Jump. And Wilbur's mine."

"And who is Wilbur?" Papa asked.

"He's a frog. I found him and he's mine." Olga said.

"And I said I was going to take Wilbur to the Frog Jump and she punched me," Henry said.

"I wish I hadn't done it," Olga said, "I'm sorry."

Papa considered the matter.

"I think it's proper for Olga to allow Henry to enter Wilbur in the contest, and it's fair that he divide with her if he wins. We'll all go to the celebration together."

"Will he divide half and half?" Olga asked.

"Half and half," Papa answered.

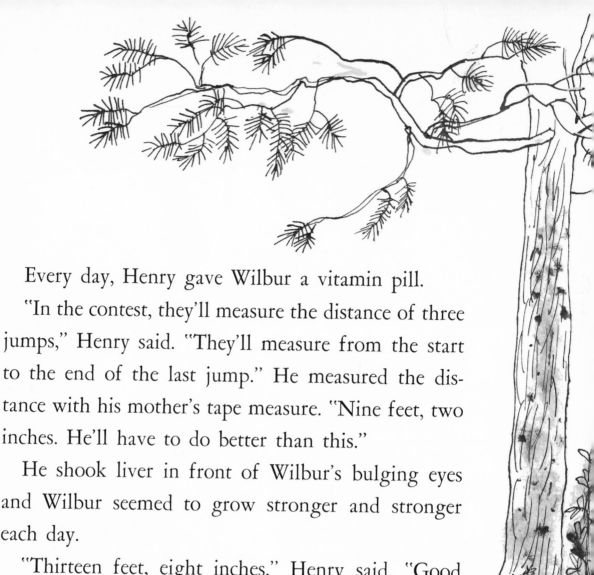

Every day, Henry gave Wilbur a vitamin pill.

"In the contest, they'll measure the distance of three jumps," Henry said. "They'll measure from the start to the end of the last jump." He measured the distance with his mother's tape measure. "Nine feet, two inches. He'll have to do better than this."

He shook liver in front of Wilbur's bulging eyes and Wilbur seemed to grow stronger and stronger each day.

"Thirteen feet, eight inches," Henry said. "Good old Wilbur."

"What prize will we win?" Olga asked.

"Three hundred for first prize or two hundred for second."

"Dollars or pennies?" Olga asked.

"Beans," said Henry.

"Dollars," said their mother, as she rolled up her tape measure.

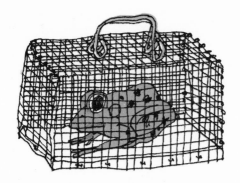

When the entry blank came for the Frog Jump, Papa read the rules.

"There's no charge for boys and girls under twelve. That's good. We'll start when I get home from work Friday, and we'll camp overnight by the Stanislaus River. We can be at the fair early on Saturday."

"There's nothing I like better than a sleep-out," Henry said.

"I saw by the newspaper that they're expecting people to bring over fifteen hundred frogs," said Papa.

"And not one will be as good as Wilbur," Olga boasted.

Henry made a wire carrying cage for Wilbur, and Olga waited impatiently for the day when they could start.

At last the day came.

When Papa arrived home from work, they were all ready to go except Henry, who had gone to get Wilbur.

"Put this basket on the back seat of the car," Mama said. "This is our supper for tonight. And these cartons have food for tomorrow. They can go in the trunk. There's no place more beautiful for camping than along the Stanislaus River."

Her father put the sleeping bags in the back of the car.

"Where's Henry?" Papa said. He raised his voice. "HENRY!"

Henry called back from the vacant lot. "I can't find him."

"You can't find WILBUR?" Papa said.

"You ALWAYS find Wilbur," Mama called.

Olga shoved open the screen door and was already ducking under the fence, when it slammed behind her.

Wilbur wasn't in the old tub. She listened for his deep, rumbling croak, but she heard only the birds cheeping in the apricot trees.

She looked in their own yard, under the damp ferns that grew in the cool, narrow passageway at the side of the house, but he wasn't there either.

She listened again. A croak came from somewhere back of the house. She ran in the direction of the sound, and there was Wilbur, sitting in a small puddle made by slow little drips from the garden hose.

"I've found him," she called.

"Nice going," said Papa. "Then I guess we're ready."

Henry put Wilbur in his carrying cage and set him on the back seat of the car. He added a jar of liver to the picnic basket.

"Everyone in?" Papa asked. "Fasten your seat belts, please. We are about to take off."

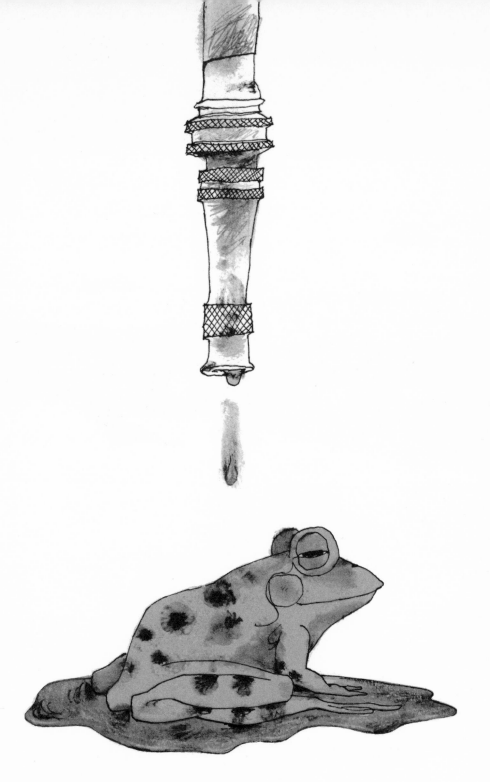

They rolled along the highway and Olga was really hungry by the time they turned off to follow the river road. They all watched for a good place to stop.

Eventually, they found a place where they could pull off the road and park under the oak trees. Here, the river was wide, and clear shallow pools were caught between the smooth rocks near the bank.

Olga supervised while Papa unpacked the trunk and lifted the picnic basket from the car, and unrolled the sleeping bags.

"I think Henry and I will take a look around," said Papa.

"And Olga and I will have supper set out when you get back," Mama said.

Olga set Wilbur's carrying cage in the cool shade and poked a finger through the wire mesh. "I don't think he likes being cooped up."

"He probably smells the river," Mama said.

"What's the matter, Wilbur?" Olga opened the little door and reached for him, and Wilbur made the longest jump of his life.

He landed with a loud plop in the river.

"What was that?" Mama asked.

"That was Wilbur," Olga answered. "He's in the river. Look. He's on a rock. Maybe I'd better get him."

Mama looked at the water. "It's shallow. Wade out slowly and don't go beyond the rock."

Olga waded out calling softly. "It's me . . . Olga. Wait for me, Wilbur."

Wilbur flicked out his tongue and wrapped it around a mosquito. "Good boy," Olga said. Slowly she reached for him —

"I CAUGHT HIM!" she shouted.

Henry came running along the bank. "What did you catch?" he yelled.

"WILBUR!" she said triumphantly.

"Mama," Henry said. "What's Wilbur doing out there? Did she let him out of the cage?"

"Never mind," Papa said. "Just see that he's put in again."

That night, they ate almost everything in the picnic basket — ham sandwiches, stuffed eggs, bananas. And afterward, they climbed into their sleeping bags.

Olga lay there and listened to the birds chirping sleepily in the willow trees, and to the frogs croaking in the river, and Wilbur answering from his carrying cage.

Olga closed her eyes, and when she opened them again, it was morning.

Mama fried bacon and eggs over a little campfire and then they climbed into the car and headed up the road for the fair.

Papa paid the entrance fee for himself and Mama,
and Henry and Olga went in free.

People were everywhere and they were with and
without frogs. There was laughing and shouting.

They stopped to watch a shooting contest.

A girl pulled a gun from its holster and shot a balloon target before Olga could blink an eye.

"She's quick on the draw," said Papa.

They saw dogs herding sheep.

The dogs circled around the sheep and herded them
through a gate.

"Fine dogs," said Papa.

They listened to a banjo band.

Then they were ready for the Frog Jumps.

"Time for the preliminary jumps," a judge said.

Olga waited for them to call Wilbur's number. They all stood beside a frog arena and watched a boy set his frog on a little felt pad on the jump mat.

The boy shouted and the frog jumped. The judges
watched the frog jump three times.

Olga watched frogs jumping and judges measuring
until it was Wilbur's turn.

When Wilbur's number was called, Henry stepped over and set Wilbur on the jump mat. Then, Henry clenched his fists, bent his knees and jumped straight up in the air behind Wilbur. Henry came down hard, but Wilbur didn't move.

Henry tried again. He landed with a tremendous thud, but Wilbur remained motionless.

"What's the matter with him?" a judge asked.

"Try again," said another.

Wilbur didn't blink an eye.

"Disqualified," said a judge. "I'm sorry."

"Take him," Henry said to Olga. "He's YOUR frog."

"That means he can't jump for the prize, doesn't it?" Olga asked.

"That's right," Papa answered.

Olga put Wilbur in his cage and walked back to the parking lot with him. She put him on the back seat and rummaged around in the papers in the picnic basket and found the jar of liver. She dangled a piece in front of him, but he wasn't interested.

"HURRY," Henry called. "There's a lot to see —"

They looked at everything: fat cows, sleek horses, woolly sheep.

They watched a man shoe a horse, and another man riding a Brahma bull. Olga held her breath.

There were hot dogs and balloons and whistles and
peanuts and fresh popcorn.

And at the end of the day, they all drove back to the river.

"This is almost the best part," Henry said, as they pulled off the road and parked under the oak trees.

Olga touched her father's sleeve.

"Papa," she said. "Wilbur is MY frog. I think he likes the smell of the river. I'd like to turn him loose here."

Papa looked at Henry. "What do you say, Henry?"

"It's all right with me," Henry said.

Olga carried Wilbur's cage to the edge of the water, and opened the door.

Wilbur hesitated only a moment.

"WOW," said Henry. "Look at that jump."

Olga closed the cage door. "Good-bye, Wilbur," she said.

Their father built a campfire and they sat around
it together, smelling the good smoke, feeling the cool
wind that blew over the river. Olga looked up at the
stars and thought about the first prize. Three hundred
dollars, and Henry would have given half of it to her.

"How much is half of nothing?" she asked.

No one answered, so she figured it out for herself.

"Half of nothing is nothing," she said. "And that's what's we started out with, so Henry and I didn't lose anything. Wilbur is the one who got a prize. He won the whole Stanislaus River."

And in the river, it seemed as if a million, trillion frogs croaked, and she was almost sure she could hear Wilbur, the loudest and deepest and most rumbling of them all.

The Author

PATRICIA MILES MARTIN and her husband live in San Mateo, California, where she writes six days a week in a pantry-turned-office. She describes herself as a "compulsive writer," having had her first poem accepted by a newspaper in Monette, Missouri, when she was seven years old. Now she reviews children's books in several well-known newspapers throughout the United States.

Mrs. Martin wrote poetry until 1957, and then started writing fiction for young people. She has been most successful and has had more than a dozen books published for young people.

The Artist

EARL THOLLANDER was born in Kingsburg, California, and educated in San Francisco. He began serious training as an artist at the City College of San Francisco and subsequently attended various colleges for art training. Mr. Thollander is an avid traveler and he especially enjoys working "on location." For a recent book, *No, No, Rosina,* also written by Patricia Miles Martin, he spent a day sailing out to sea in a crab-fishing boat. For this book he attended the Frog Jump Jubilee with his family. Mr. Thollander, his wife, and their two children live in a house which overlooks San Francisco Bay.